Courtesy
Is Kindness

By Huda Essa
Illustrated by Violet Tobacco

Publishing Credits

Rachelle Cracchiolo, M.S.Ed., *Publisher*
Emily R. Smith, M.A.Ed., *VP of Content Development*
Véronique Bos, *Creative Director*
Dani Neiley, *Associate Editor*
Kevin Pham, *Graphic Designer*

Image Credits

Illustrated by Violet Tobacco

Library of Congress Cataloging-in-Publication Data

Names: Essa, Huda, author. | Tobacco, Violet, illustrator.
Title: Courtesy is kindness / by Huda Essa ; illustrated by Violet
 Tobacco.
Description: Huntington Beach, CA : Teacher Created Materials,
 [2022] | Audience: Grades 2-3. | Summary: "Omar finds joy in
 looking for ways people show courtesy. Kindness is all
 around!"-- Provided by publisher.
Identifiers: LCCN 2021051081 (print) | LCCN 2021051082 (ebook) |
 ISBN 9781087601748 (paperback) | ISBN 9781087631752 (ebook)
Subjects: LCSH: Readers (Primary) | LCGFT: Readers (Publications)
Classification: LCC PE1119.2 .E873 2022 (print) | LCC PE1119.2
 (ebook) | DDC 428.6/2--dc23/eng/20211102
LC record available at https://lccn.loc.gov/2021051081
LC ebook record available at https://lccn.loc.gov/2021051082

TCM Teacher Created Materials

5482 Argosy Avenue
Huntington Beach, CA 92649
www.tcmpub.com

ISBN 978-1-0876-0174-8

Printed in Malaysia. THU001.46774

Table of Contents

Chapter One

✿

Starting with Goodbye

"See you tomorrow!" Omar shouted. Omar waved goodbye to Malik as he got in the car. He had so much fun at Malik's house. Sadly, it was time to go home.

Omar got in the car and pulled on his seat belt. "All set, Dad!" he said as he buckled himself in.

Omar looked out his window. Malik was still standing on the sidewalk, watching them get ready to leave. Omar was surprised to see Malik still standing there.

He wondered whether something was wrong, but it didn't look like anything was going on.

Malik smiled and waved again to Omar and his dad. Omar's dad honked the horn when they drove away.

As they got to the end of the block, Omar saw Malik walk inside his house.

"Why did Malik stay to watch us leave?" Omar asked.

"People show courtesy in many ways," his dad explained. "Malik waited and watched to make sure that we left safely. He was showing us courtesy."

Omar smiled to himself. *Malik must care about us*, he thought.

Chapter Two

✿

All Kinds of Answers

Learning about Malik's kindness made Omar curious. He thought for a few minutes.

"How else do people show courtesy?" he asked his dad.

"There are answers all around," Omar's dad replied. "You just have to look for them."

On their way home, Omar and his dad stopped at the store. Omar's dad held the door open for Omar. He held the door open for other people, too. Most of them smiled and said *thank you*.

Omar's dad winked at him. Omar knew that these were more ways to show courtesy.

When they got home, Omar saw even more ways to show courtesy. Omar's mom came to help carry in the grocery bags.

He did not want to forget the ways he could show courtesy, so he found some paper and made a list.

Chapter Three

✿

Courtesy All Around

Omar saw more ways to show courtesy the next day at school.

In the morning, Omar's pencil broke in math class. Delma let him use one of hers. Later, Moussa let Lan borrow his book. He knew she liked to read, too. In gym class, Jeneen lost her ring while playing tag. Dean stopped playing to help her find it. During centers, Ty looked too shy to ask to play with the other kids, so Maggie asked him to join her game.

Omar heard words such as *please* and *thank you*. He also heard *excuse me* and *you're welcome*.

Some students showed courtesy without using words. Sam helped a new student find her class when she was lost.

Teachers showed courtesy as well. Ms. Soto stayed late to help Lan find her glasses. And Mr. Green stayed after class to help Dean with his homework. Omar's list was getting long.

Omar wanted to try showing courtesy, too. While walking toward the playground, he saw a ball that had been kicked off the soccer field. It landed far away from the players but not too far from him.

He ran and kicked it toward the soccer players. They smiled, waved, and yelled "Thank you!" Helping people felt great!

On the playground, Marco fell off the monkey bars. Omar stopped what he was doing to rush over and help him up. Marco didn't say thank you or smile at Omar. He just ran back to his friends. *It's strange that Marco didn't thank me for being kind to him,* Omar thought to himself.

Chapter Four

✿

Spreading Kindness

A few days later, Omar was playing outside with friends. He slipped and fell in some mud. A few of the other kids laughed. Omar began to feel upset. Some of the same people he helped were now laughing at him for falling! It didn't seem fair. Tears began to fill his eyes.

Then, he looked up and saw a hand reaching out to help him up. It was Marco!

"Thanks, Marco! I can't believe I fell in the mud. How embarrassing!" Omar said.

"Don't worry. Everyone falls down sometimes. You helped me when I fell off the monkey bars. I'm happy I could return the favor." Marco smiled at Omar and ran back to his game.

As Omar thought about the past few days, he smiled. Marco had recognized Omar's kindness on the playground after all. He just showed it in a different way. Omar felt proud to be able to help spread kindness. His new goal was to find a way to show courtesy each day.

About Us

The Author
Huda Essa used to be a teacher of children. Now, she teaches teachers. She is also the author of *Teach Us Your Name* and *Common Threads: Adam's Day at the Market*.

The Illustrator
Violet Tobacco is an illustrator from Atlanta, Georgia. She grew up drawing and performing in theater groups. She loves illustrating children's books, portraits, character designs, and concept work.